Give the
Dog a Bone

ALLAN AHLBERG • ANDRÉ AMSTUTZ

PUFFIN

On a dark dark hill
in a dark dark garden
there is a little bony dog . . .

without a bone.

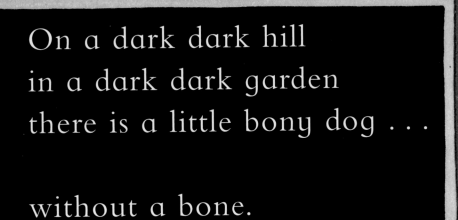

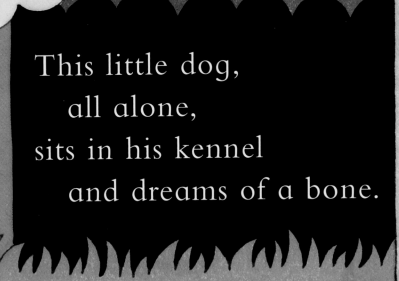

This little dog,
all alone,
sits in his kennel
and dreams of a bone.

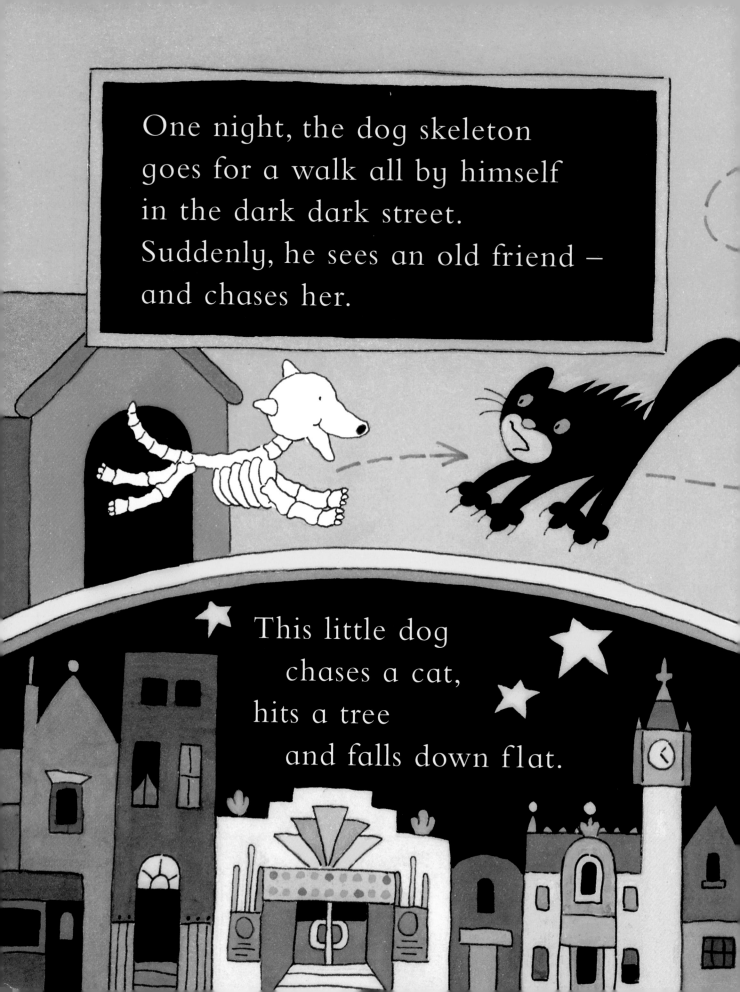

One night, the dog skeleton goes for a walk all by himself in the dark dark street. Suddenly, he sees an old friend – and chases her.

This little dog
chases a cat,
hits a tree
and falls down flat.

The dog skeleton
loses a bit of himself
but keeps walking.
He comes to the dark dark park
and swings on the swings
and slides on the slide.

He chases the ducks
on the dark dark pond . . .
and loses another bit!

This little dog
chases a duck,
loses a leg –
what rotten luck!

The dog skeleton
hops out of the dark dark park,
down the dark dark street
and into the dark dark pet shop.

Suddenly, he sees some more old friends . . .

and they chase *him*.

This little dog
slips and slides.
Can anyone here
see where he hides?

Off goes the dog,
away from the pet shop,
away from the pets
and away from himself.
(He's lost another bit!)

The dog skeleton
hops up the street
and over the hill
and down the street
and round the corner.

Suddenly, he meets *another* old friend . . . and *plays* with him.

This little dog
   chases a friend,
loses his tail –
   is this the end?

Bits of him gone.
Lost in the fog.
Can anyone see
what's left of the dog?

No, they can't.
The big skeleton
on his bike can't,
and the little *skeleton*
on his bike can't.
Look out!

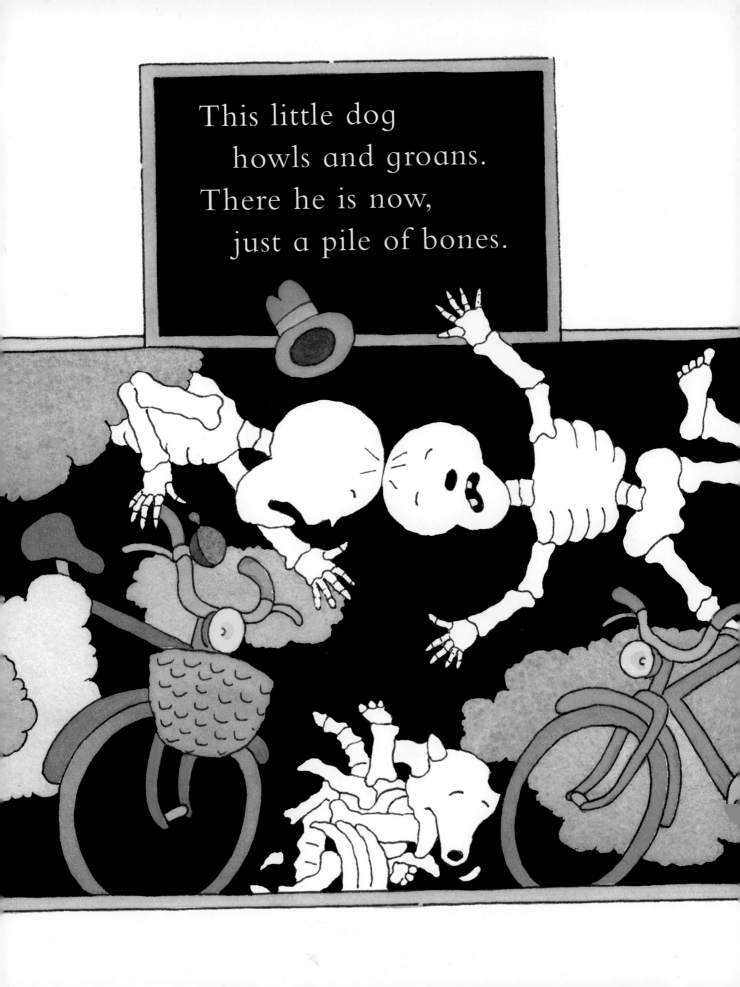

This little dog
howls and groans.
There he is now,
just a pile of bones.

But not for long.
Soon the big skeleton
and the little skeleton
gather him up.

They follow the trail
of his lost bones,
along the street,
into the pet shop,
into the park . . .
and back home.

Then they put him together again.
"His legs are on wrong," says Little.
"Wofo!" barks the dog.
"His tail is on wrong," says Big.
"Owof!" barks the dog.
"His head is on wrong," say Little *and* Bi

At last the dog skeleton
is himself again.
"Woof-woof!" he barks,
and trots off on *four* legs
to his kennel.

On a dark dark hill
in a dark dark garden
there is a little bony dog . . .

The End

PUFFIN BOOKS

Published by the Penguin Group
Penguin Books Ltd, 80 Strand, London WC2R 0RL, England
Penguin Group (USA) Inc., 375 Hudson Street, New York, New York 10014, USA
Penguin Group (Canada), 10 Alcorn Avenue, Toronto, Ontario, Canada M4V 3B2
(a division of Pearson Penguin Canada Inc.)
Penguin Ireland, 25 St Stephen's Green, Dublin 2, Ireland (a division of Penguin Books Ltd)
Penguin Group (Australia), 250 Camberwell Road, Camberwell, Victoria 3124, Australia
(a division of Pearson Australia Group Pty Ltd)
Penguin Books India Pvt Ltd, 11 Community Centre, Panchsheel Park, New Delhi – 110 017, India
Penguin Group (NZ), cnr Airborne and Rosedale Roads, Albany, Auckland 1310, New Zealand
(a division of Pearson New Zealand Ltd)
Penguin Books (South Africa) (Pty) Ltd, 24 Sturdee Avenue, Rosebank, Johannesburg 2196, South Africa

Penguin Books Ltd, Registered Offices: 80 Strand, London WC2R 0RL, England

puffinbooks.com

First published by William Heinemann Ltd 1993
First published in Puffin Books 2005
004 - 10 9 8 7 6 5 4

Text copyright © Allan Ahlberg, 1993
Illustrations copyright © André Amstutz, 1993
All rights reserved

The moral right of the author and illustrator has been asserted

Set in Bembo
Manufactured in China

British Library Cataloguing in Publication Data
A CIP catalogue record for this book is available from the British Library

ISBN 978-0-14056-686-4